An I Can Read Book™

Detective Dinosaur LOST AND FOUND

by JAMES SKOFIELD

pictures by R. W. ALLEY

HarperCollins*Publishers*

For Michael, Gracie, Cooter,
and little Maggie
—J.S.

For the young authors and
illustrators of Sowams School
—R.W.A.

Detective Dinosaur
Lost and Found

For information address HarperCollins Children's
Books, a division of HarperCollins Publishers,
10 East 53rd Street, New York, NY 10022.
Manufactured in China.

Library of Congress Cataloging-in-Publication Data
Skofield, James.
Detective Dinosaur : lost and found / story by James Skofield ; pictures by R. W. Alley.
p. cm. — (An I can read book)
Summary: After Detective Dinosaur and Officer Pterodactyl find a missing baby and a home for Cadet Kitty, they lose and find each other.
ISBN 0-06-026784-4. — ISBN 0-06-026785-2 (lib. bdg.) — ISBN 0-06-444257-8 (pbk.)
[1. Dinosaurs—Fiction. 2. Lost and found possessions—Fiction. 3. Mystery and detective stories.] I. Alley, R. W. (Robert W.), ill. II. Title. III. Series.
PZ7.S62835Dg 1998 97-2725
[E]—DC21 CIP
AC

11 12 13 SCP 20 19 18 17 16 15

❖

Contents

Dinosaurs in the story

Pterodactyl	(ter-eh-DAK-tul)
Apatosaurus	(a-pah-teh-SOR-us)
Velociraptor	(veh-LA-seh-rap-ter)
Iguanodon	(i-GWA-neh-don)
Maiasaur	(MAY-a-sor)
Tyrannosaurus	(tih-ran-uh-SAW-russ)

Detective Dinosaur

and Officer Pterodactyl

were on patrol.

"Help!" called Granny Apatosaurus.

"Baby Penny is lost!"

"Do not worry, Granny,"

said Detective Dinosaur.

"We will find her."

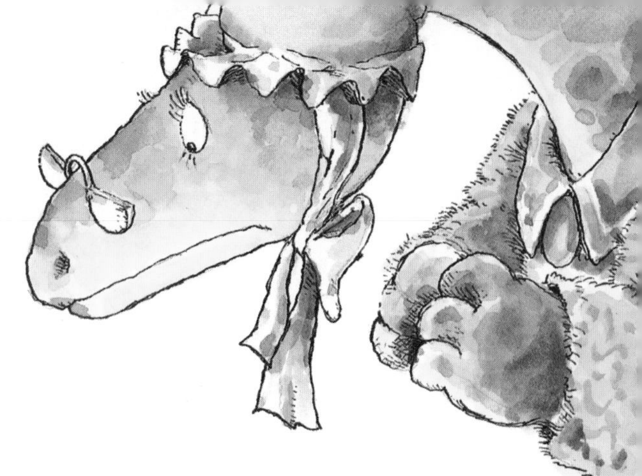

"Is she wearing a pink diaper?"
asked Vinnie Velociraptor.
"Yes," said Granny Apatosaurus.
"She took my taxi
and headed for the park,"
said Vinnie.

"Oh dear," said Detective Dinosaur.

"We have a lost baby

who has stolen a taxi.

We must find her!"

Two blocks away

Inez Iguanodon lay in the street.

"A baby ran me over!" she cried.

"Oh dear, oh dear,"

said Detective Dinosaur.

"Penny is a lost baby

who has stolen a taxi

and has run over Inez."

At the park gate two Maiasaurs
sat in a hot-air balloon basket.
"A baby grabbed our balloon!"
they said.
"Come with us,"
said Officer Pterodactyl.

Inside the park
they found the taxi in a mud puddle.
They found the hot-air balloon in a tree.
They found the pink diaper on the grass.
But they did not find
Baby Penny.

“We will split up
and look for her,”
said Detective Dinosaur.
“Meet back here by that big rock.”

An hour later

Baby Penny was still lost.

"I will never see Baby Penny again,"

said Granny Apatosaurus.

Suddenly the rock moved.

"Earthquake!"

yelled Detective Dinosaur.

"Hello, Granny," said the rock.

It was Baby Penny!

"Let's play hide-and-seek,"

she said.

"No, no, no!"

said Detective Dinosaur.

"You are going to the police station.

You are a lost baby

who stole a taxi,

ran over Inez,

and took a balloon.

And now you have no diaper on!"

Tears filled Baby Penny's eyes.

"Hold on, sir,"

said Officer Pterodactyl.

"Do not cry, Baby Penny," she said.

"Are you sorry you ran away?"

"I'm sorry," said Baby Penny.

"Will you give everything back?"

asked Officer Pterodactyl.

Baby Penny nodded.

She gave back the taxi.

She gave back the hot-air balloon.

Everyone helped put the pink diaper back on Baby Penny.

"Are we going to the police station?" asked Granny Apatosaurus.

"No," said Detective Dinosaur.

"Baby Penny gave back the taxi.

She gave back the balloon.

She is wearing her diaper.

She is no longer lost,

but please don't lose her again!"

POLICE

One night Detective Dinosaur
and Officer Pterodactyl
heard a strange sound.
It came from the garage.
Slowly they opened the garage door.

They saw a brown paper bag.

It was moving!

“Is it an alligator?”

asked Detective Dinosaur.

"It is too small to be an alligator, sir," said Officer Pterodactyl.

"Meow," said the paper bag.

Detective Dinosaur jumped.

"A snake!" he cried.

“I do not think so, sir,”

said Officer Pterodactyl.

She reached into the paper bag

and pulled out a kitten.

“What is a kitten doing here?”

asked Detective Dinosaur.

“I think she is lost, sir,”

said Officer Pterodactyl.

They gave the kitten some milk.

Then the kitten went to sleep.

The next day they put up signs:

HAVE YOU LOST THIS KITTEN?

CALL THE POLICE STATION.

They waited days

and weeks

and months,

but no one called.

"Poor lost kitty,"

said Detective Dinosaur.

VE YOU
ST THIS
TTEN?
LL THE
E STATION

One evening Chief Tyrannosaurus
could not find his keys.

Everybody looked for them.

They looked in lockers.

They looked under desks.

“Where are my keys?”

yelled Chief Tyrannosaurus.

Just then the kitten
dragged the keys into the room.

"Well done, kitty!" said the Chief.

"What is your name?"

"She does not have a name, Chief,"

said Detective Dinosaur.

"She is a lost kitty."

"Nonsense," said the Chief.

"She is a found kitty.

She found my keys!

I will call her Cadet Kitty."

Cadet Kitty purred loudly.

"I guess she isn't

a poor lost kitty after all,"

said Detective Dinosaur.

"We found her."

"Or," said Officer Pterodactyl,

"maybe she found us."

Detective Dinosaur,

Officer Pterodactyl,

and Cadet Kitty were on night patrol

in the park.

It was dark and foggy.

Suddenly they heard a noise.

"Who goes there?"

called Detective Dinosaur.

There was no reply.

"I had better take a look,"

Detective Dinosaur said.

He followed the noise

for a long time.

At last he shouted,

"I am tired of following you.

Come out in the name of the law!"

Something hopped out of the bushes.

“Oh, it is only a bunny,”
said Detective Dinosaur.
“You had better hop home.
It is very late.”

Detective Dinosaur started back,
but the fog was very thick,
and soon he was lost.

Officer Pterodactyl
and Cadet Kitty were worried.
"Detective Dinosaur, where are you?"
called Officer Pterodactyl.
There was no reply.

Detective Dinosaur

sat down on a tree stump.

He was cold and wet and tired.

He felt like crying.

“This will never do,” he said.

“I am a police detective.

I must be brave.

Maybe if I sing

I will feel better.”

Detective Dinosaur sang:

"I helped find Baby Penny.

I found a little kitty.

I cannot find my way now.

Oh drat! It is a pity!

I like summer sunshine.

I like snow and ice.

I do not like this clammy fog.

I'm lost! This is not nice!"

Suddenly he heard,

"Detective Dinosaur!"

It was Officer Pterodactyl.

"Over here! Over here!"

shouted Detective Dinosaur.

"Thank goodness we found you,"

said Officer Pterodactyl.

Back at the police station
they all drank hot soup.
"It was no fun being lost,"
said Detective Dinosaur.
"How did you find me?"
"Oh, sir," said Officer Pterodactyl.
"You are a good dinosaur.
You are a brave detective.
But you sing so loudly,
it was easy to find you."

CASSIE
+
MAX

“Found or lost,

lost and found,

I have the loudest

voice around,”

sang Detective Dinosaur.

“Yes, sir!” said Officer Pterodactyl,

and Cadet Kitty just purred.